The Tiara Club

at Pearl Palace

For the lovely Princess Grace,
of London
VF

www.tiaraclub.co.uk

ORCHARD BOOKS
338 Euston Road, London NW1 3BH
Orchard Books Australia
Level 17/207 Kent St, Sydney, NSW 2000
A Paperback Original
First published in 2007 by Orchard Books

Text © Vivian French 2007
Cover illustration © Sarah Gibb 2007
Inside illustrations © Orchard Books 2007

A CIP catalogue record for this book is available
from the British Library.

ISBN 978 1 84616 501 6

1 3 5 7 9 10 8 6 4 2

Printed in Great Britain

The paper and board used in this paperback are natural recyclable
products made from wood grown in sustainable forests.
The manufacturing processes conform to the environmental
regulations of the country of origin.

Orchard Books is a division of Hachette Children's Books,
an Hachette Livre UK company.

www.orchardbooks.co.uk

The Tiara Club

at Pearl Palace

Princess Grace

and the Golden Nightingale

By Vivian French

ORCHARD BOOKS

The Royal Palace Academy
for the Preparation of Perfect Princesses

(Known to our students as "*The Princess Academy*")

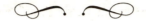

OUR SCHOOL MOTTO:
*A Perfect Princess always thinks of others
before herself, and is kind, caring and truthful.*

**Pearl Palace offers a complete education for
Tiara Club princesses with emphasis on the arts
and outdoor activities. The curriculum includes:**

*A special Princess
Sports Day*

*A trip to the Magical
Mountains*

*Preparation for the
Silver Swan Award
(stories and poems)*

*A visit to the King
Rudolfo's Exhibition of
Musical Instruments*

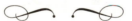

**Our headteacher, King Everest, is present at all times,
and students are well looked after by the head fairy
godmother, Fairy G, and her assistant, Fairy Angora.**

Our resident staff and visiting experts include:

*QUEEN MOLLY
(Sports and games)*

*LADY MALVEENA
(Secretary to King Everest)*

*LORD HENRY
(Natural History)*

*QUEEN MOTHER MATILDA
(Etiquette, Posture and
Flower Arranging)*

We award tiara points to encourage our Tiara Club princesses towards the next level. All princesses who win enough points at Pearl Palace will be presented with their Pearl Sashes and attend a celebration ball.

Pearl Sash Tiara Club princesses are invited to go on to Emerald Castle, our very special residence for Perfect Princesses, where they may continue their education at a higher level.

PLEASE NOTE:
Pets are not allowed at Pearl Palace.
Princesses are expected to arrive at
the Academy with a *minimum* of:

TWENTY BALLGOWNS
(with all necessary hoops,
petticoats, etc)

TWELVE DAY DRESSES

SEVEN GOWNS
suitable for garden parties,
and other special
day occasions

TWELVE TIARAS

DANCING SHOES
five pairs

VELVET SLIPPERS
three pairs

RIDING BOOTS
two pairs

Cloaks, muffs, stoles, gloves
and other essential
accessories as required

Hello, lovely princess.
I'm Princess Grace, and
I think you might have already
met Hannah, Isabella, Lucy, Ellie
and Sarah - we share Lily Room,
and it's wonderful! Just imagine
sharing with Diamonde and
Gruella - you'd probably find
toads in your shoes or spiders
in your slippers. Oooh!
Wouldn't that be AWFUL?

Chapter One

One of the lovely things about being at Pearl Palace is that we have really interesting lessons. We do get the usual boring ones as well, like Maths for the Modern Monarch (oof! I am SO not good at maths!) but on Fridays we have Special Topic classes, and they're FUN. We've had Spinning Wheels, and how to avoid them, Frogs, and how to tell if they're enchanted, and two whole Fridays learning how to tell Unsuitable Princes that we don't want to marry them. I thought that would be simple – I mean, don't you just say, "No, thank you"? But I was wrong. Apparently you have to be VERY kind and gracious so they don't rush off to fight dragons.

When Fairy G (she's the head fairy godmother at the Princess Academy) told us we were going to have a Special Topic lesson on Royal Artefacts, I was thrilled.

Well, I was after I discovered what artefacts are. I wasn't exactly sure – but Hannah told me they're things that tell you about how people used to live. Like ancient pottery bowls, or wooden clogs. And then she said she was going to take us to King Rudolfo the Third's private Museum of Royal Life, and we were absolutely

beside ourselves with excitement. We'd been there before when we were in Silver Towers, and it was BRILLIANT!

"I'm afraid King Rudolfo won't be there when we visit," Fairy G told us. "He's away on a royal tour – but we're invited to see his brand

new collection of musical artefacts."

"MUSICAL artefacts?" We stared at her.

Fairy G smiled her enormous smile. "There's a magic harp, and a silver flute, and a pipe that will make rats follow you—"

"YUCK!" Lucy shuddered. "We

don't have to play it, do we?"

"It's safely under lock and key," Fairy G reassured her. "But the most beautiful thing by far is the golden nightingale. King Rudolfo has it on loan from a Chinese emperor, so we're VERY lucky to see it...and guess what!"

"What? What is it, Fairy G?"

None of us could guess at all.

"King Rudolfo has allowed Pearl Palace to a musical party at his museum in the evening, and the nightingale is going to sing!"

"WOW!" Hannah spoke for us all. "That sounds AMAZING!"

But then Diamonde asked, "How can a golden nightingale sing? It's not REAL, is it?"

"It's clockwork," Fairy G explained. "It was made hundreds of years ago, and it sings as beautifully as a real bird. Nobody knows who made it, but he – or she – must have been very skilful."

"H'mph." Diamonde sounded

REALLY unimpressed. "Gruella
and I had clockwork toys when
we were babies. I don't see what's
so special about this one."

Fairy G raised her eyebrows.
"Do I understand you don't want
to come with us, Diamonde?"

Diamonde shrugged. "We'll
come," she said.

"After all, King Rudolfo IS one
of Mummy's best friends,"
Gruella added.

"But he won't be there," Fairy G
reminded her. "He's asked his son,
Prince Georgio, to show us the
musical instruments."

"Prince Georgio? REALLY?"

Diamonde and Gruella sat bolt upright. Then they suddenly realised we were looking at them, and tried to pretend they weren't bothered, but it was

too late.

Even Fairy G was chuckling as she asked, "So what's so special about this young man?"

Diamonde put her nose in the air. "Nothing."

Gruella said, "He's very nice—" and then squeaked because Diamonde pinched her.

"Well – we'll see for ourselves at the end of the week," Fairy G said cheerfully, and we went back to our lessons.

Chapter Two

We left for the Royal Museum as soon as lunch was over on Friday. Fairy G had said we could wear party dresses because we were staying for the concert, so that made us feel very special.

"Right – everybody here?" Fairy G asked as we climbed into the coaches.

"I haven't seen Diamonde and Gruella yet," Sarah said. Fairy G made a tut-tutting noise, and went to check the other coaches. She was just storming back to Pearl Palace when the front door opened, and Diamonde and Gruella tottered out.

"What are they wearing?" Isabella gasped. "They can't even walk, their shoes have got SUCH high heels."

"Prince Georgio must be really special," Ellie said with a giggle.

"I don't think Fairy G looks very pleased!" Sarah and Hannah were watching out of the other window.

"Look – she's telling them to go back inside and change...she's FURIOUS!"

It was true. Fairy G grows much, much bigger when she's angry, and she was positively enormous as she shooed Diamonde and Gruella back into the building. Of course we had to wait until the twins had changed, and that made us late starting, so Fairy G got even crosser. She was huffing and puffing by the time Diamonde and Gruella reappeared, and she told them to hurry into our coach and not waste any more time. Gruella muttered, "Sorry,

Fairy G," as she got in, but Diamonde didn't look sorry at all.

When we got to the enormous drive that led to King Rudolfo's palace Diamonde began to wriggle about, and I saw she was taking her shoes off. Then she fished in her handbag, and I saw she'd brought her extra-high heels with her, after all!

"Is that a good idea?" I asked.
"Fairy G won't be very happy—"

"Mind your own business!"
Diamonde snapped. "YOU may
not mind looking like a baby,
but I do! Mummy says I look
especially grown-up in these."

I didn't know what else to say,
so I didn't say anything. Diamonde
gave me another black look, but she
did put her super-high heels back
in her bag. "Little Miss Teacher's
Pet," she hissed. "I suppose you're
going to sneak to Fairy G!"

"Of course I won't," I said.

Diamonde shut her bag with
a snap, and grabbed Gruella.

"Come on. Let's get out of this coach. It's much too full of horrible telltales!"

It was a good thing Diamonde wasn't wearing her special heels, because Fairy G was standing right outside our coach as we got out. Beside her was a prince who looked about the same age as us,

or maybe just a little bit older. Although I don't usually notice boys much I did think he was quite handsome.

Diamonde went fiery red. "Oh, hi there, Prince Georgio!" she said in a weirdly breathless sort of voice. "Haven't seen you for AGES AND AGES!"

The prince looked surprised. "Oh...er...hello. You're...er...um... Gruella?"

Diamonde positively snorted. "NO! I mean, actually, no I'm not. I'm Diamonde. This is Gruella."

"Nice to see you both again," Prince Georgio said, but he didn't sound as if he meant it. "My dad said I was to show you the way to the summerhouse, and open the door for you. This way, please."

Diamonde immediately slipped her arm through his, and gave him a sickly smile.

"I'm SO looking forward to seeing the magic nightingale," she gushed. "Is it really as lovely as I've heard?"

Poor Prince Georgio! He was too polite to take his arm away, but he looked very uncomfortable as he said, "You mean the golden nightingale? Er...yes, I suppose it is a bit special."

Gruella pounced on his other arm. "Will you be coming to the party afterwards?" she asked him. "I DO hope you will!"

"Diamonde! Gruella!" Fairy G clapped her hands loudly, and I was sure I saw a twinkle in her eye. "Could you come back here, please? Grace, would you and Prince Georgio take my bag to the summerhouse while I take the register and make sure we haven't left anyone behind?"

Chapter Three

If looks could kill I'd have been dead, but even Diamonde didn't dare to disobey Fairy G when she spoke in that tone of voice.

"Uh oh," I thought as I walked through the museum garden beside Prince Georgio. "I wonder what she'll do now?"

Georgio gave me a sideways

smile. "That was kind of your teacher. I probably shouldn't say this, but I can't stand those twins. My dad knows their mother and they sometimes come here to visit, and they NEVER stop showing off."

"They're a bit like that at school," I told him. "I think maybe they don't have much fun at home...but I don't know."

"It's nice of you to make excuses for them." The prince smiled at me again. "Will you do me a favour? Will you make sure I don't have to dance with them at the party tonight?"

I didn't know what to say. I'd never met this boy before, and already he was acting as if he'd known me for ages.

"Er...I'll do my best," I said. "Tell you what, I'll talk to my friends. There are six of us in Lily

Room, and we could take turns to dance with you, if you like."

"Phew!" Prince Georgio looked MUCH more cheerful. "That would be GREAT! I was terrified I'd be stuck with the twins all evening." He stopped at the summerhouse and unlocked a big wooden door. "Here's the exhibition. Do you want a quick look at the golden nightingale before the others arrive?"

I didn't answer – I was SO surprised by the inside of the summerhouse. It was quite small, but the roof was made of glass so it was incredibly light. There were glass cases all round the walls full of weird and wonderful musical instruments – but in the very centre of the room was a round marble table, and on it was a golden cage.

Prince Georgio fished in his pocket and pulled out a golden key. Bending over the cage he wound something up – I could hear a clicking noise – and then stood back.

"Listen to that!" he said proudly...and after just half a minute I began to cry.

Why was I crying?

I don't know.

It sounds so silly when I say that, but it's true. It was the music – it was so utterly utterly beautiful – but it wasn't because it was sad. I think it was because it was so perfect. I'd never ever heard anything like it.

"I'm so sorry," I sniffed as I looked round for a hankie.

Prince Georgio gave me a cheeky grin. "I knew it would. Nice people always cry their eyes out the first time they hear it.

Just wait until tonight when I wind it up properly for the concert. We'll need a mop and a bucket by the time it's finished!"

That made me laugh, and I was still laughing as Fairy G came

stamping through the door with all the Pearl Palace students behind her. Diamonde and Gruella flew to Prince Georgio's side, and I saw him frown as they clutched his arms.

"DO show us the nightingale, Georgy darling!" Diamonde begged. "Please please pretty please with cherries on the top!"

"Make it play!" Gruella gave him the soppiest smile. "You played it for Grace, so play it for little me!"

Prince Georgio looked at Fairy G. "Would you like me to wind it up again, Madam Fairy?"

"We'll wait until the concert tonight," Fairy G said firmly, "but thank you for asking. And I'm sure you've got plenty of things to be getting on with, so please don't feel you have to stay here while we have our Special Topic lesson."

I've never heard such a huge sigh of relief. Prince Georgio gave Fairy G the widest smile, and disentangled himself from Diamonde and Gruella as quickly as he could. As he moved away

41

from the marble table I saw the little golden key lying by the nightingale's cage – and then Diamonde's hand shot out and took it.

She was so quick I almost thought I'd imagined it. I stared at her, wondering what on earth I should do – but then I caught Prince Georgio's eye, and he gave me the tiniest of winks, and put his finger to his lips.

He'd seen her take the key as well. And he didn't want me to say anything!

I'm hopeless at winking, so I gave him a little smile.

"I'll see you all at the party tonight," he said cheerfully. "The orchestra will play a few tunes, then the nightingale will sing, and finally we'll turn it into a proper party with lots of dancing!" He gave me a cheerful wave. "See you for the first dance, Princess Grace!" And then he was gone.

Chapter Four

I didn't have time to tell my
friends about dancing with
Georgio because Fairy G launched
straight into her lesson. We
were shown all the different
instruments, and she told us about
princes who had been enchanted
by musical instruments, and
princesses who had calmed

horrible savage beasts by playing the harp or the flute...and lots of other stories as well. It was really interesting, even though Diamonde kept trying to squeeze in beside me. And a couple of times I thought I heard something tapping on the glass roof, but when I looked up there was nothing there.

Fairy G ended by showing us the golden nightingale. "It's one of the musical wonders of the world," she told us. "If you listened to a real nightingale, and then to this one, you'd never be able to tell which was which. The only difference is that a real nightingale sings a slightly different song each time, whereas this one is always the same."

"It isn't very pretty," Gruella said as she looked at the little bird in the cage.

"Real nightingales are even plainer." Fairy G smiled at Gruella. "Sometimes a very plain outside can hide a beautiful secret."

Diamonde sniffed. "I'd MUCH rather be beautiful on the outside."

Fairy G gave her a strange look, but before she could say anything there was a knock on the door, and Prince Georgio hurried in. He looked as if he'd been climbing trees, or working in the garden – his hair was on end, and his clothes were covered in dirt.

As he passed me he half-tripped, and if I hadn't been in the way he'd have fallen flat on his face. As he straightened up I saw he'd left several large smears of mud on my dress.

"Oops!" he said. "I'm SO sorry – that's terrible! Oh dear! You'd better come back with me, and we'll ask the housekeeper if she can clean it!"

"It's OK," I said, and I tried to brush the mud off.

"No, no – I insist!" He gave me a quick nudge with his elbow, then turned to Fairy G and gave her a little bow. "The housekeeper asked me to tell you that tea will be ready in five minutes, Madam Fairy. I'll make sure Princess Grace's dress is OK, and then we'll see you all in the banqueting hall. We're serving tea there, if that's all right."

"Thank you." Fairy G's eyes were twinkling as Georgio steered me out of the summerhouse. Diamonde and Gruella looked like thunderclouds.

As soon as we were outside Georgio grabbed my hand. "Look in your pocket!" he whispered.

"What?" I stood still in the middle of the path, and stared at him. I was beginning to think he was completely mad.

"Go on! PLEASE!" He looked so anxious that I sighed, and fished in my pocket – and nearly collapsed in amazement.

"It's the golden key!" I gasped.

Georgio smiled very proudly. "I KNEW Diamonde was up to something as soon as I saw her take it. I climbed up on the glass roof to watch – and I saw her slip it into your pocket!"

"B-but..." I stuttered. "Why... why would she DO that?"

Georgio shrugged. "I'd say she doesn't like you very much."

I handed him the key, and we began to walk back to the palace. "Thank you VERY much," I said. "I'd have felt AWFUL if I'd found it there."

Georgio grinned at me. "I think Diamonde and Gruella have some kind of plan. But don't worry! So have I. Don't say a word to anyone about the key! Promise?"

"OK," I said.

"Good!" he gave me another wink. "Now, let's get tidied up."

"I promised I'd ask you all to take turns dancing with him," I explained. "Is that OK?"

Isabella giggled. "Do you think Diamonde and Gruella will let us? You know how good they are at barging in!"

"We'll have to make sure one of

Chapter Five

The housekeeper managed to get almost all the mud off my dress, but she sent Prince Georgio to have a bath and change his clothes, and I didn't see him again before tea. I found my way to the banqueting hall, and while we were eating I told my friends in Lily Room about Georgio's problem with the twins.

us is always ready to take over at the end of each dance," Hannah said. "Oh – look! Here he is now!"

Hannah was right. Prince Georgio came sauntering into the hall, and to my surprise he went straight over to the twins. They fluttered their eyelashes like mad.

"DO sit beside me, Georgy dear!" Diamonde said.

"NO! Sit beside ME!" Gruella pushed her sister out of the way.

Prince Georgio bowed in the most princely manner. "I'll sit next to you both," he said, and settled himself between them.

A moment later a page came running into the room. He rushed over to Georgio, and whispered urgently in his ear. The prince frowned, stood up, and went to speak to Fairy G. She listened carefully, looking more and more horrified.

"Pearl Palace Princesses!" she boomed. "Please PLEASE think back to when you were in King Rudolfo's summerhouse. This is MOST important. Did any of you see a key lying around? A little golden key?"

Nobody said anything. I could feel myself beginning to blush, and I SO hoped no one was looking at me.

Diamonde put her hand up. "Please, Fairy G – is it the key for the nightingale?"

"It is," Fairy G said. "Why – have you seen it, Diamonde?"

Diamonde shook her head. "I haven't, Fairy G, but Grace might have. She and Prince Georgio were listening to it just before we came in. I definitely heard a tweeting noise."

Every single head turned in my direction, and I knew I was bright red.

"So, Grace?" Fairy G was waiting for me to answer.

"Well, we did listen to the nightingale," I said slowly, "but I don't know what happened to the key. I'm so sorry."

"Why don't you have a look in your pocket?" Gruella's voice was very shrill.

"Why would I put it in my pocket?" I asked.

"It's there! I know it is! Isn't it, Diamonde?" Gruella pointed at me. "She wanted to get Georgy into trouble!"

Diamonde gave a silly simpering laugh. "I think you might be right, Gruella!"

Prince Georgio stepped forward. "May I suggest something, Madam Fairy?" he asked. "Might I suggest we ask Princess Grace AND the twins to empty their pockets?"

Fairy G gave Prince Georgio one of her long thoughtful stares. Then she nodded.

"That's an excellent idea."

Very slowly, I emptied my pockets. They were empty. At the exact same moment Gruella emptied hers. They were empty too. Diamonde sneered, put her hands in her pocket – and froze.

"WHAT?" she shrieked as she pulled out the little key. "WHAT? What's this doing here? I put it in GRACE'S pocket—"

And then she burst into loud noisy sobbing and ran out of the banqueting hall.

Chapter Six

I'm not sure that I really REALLY think Georgio should have slipped the key back into Diamonde's pocket, but Hannah and Sarah don't agree with me. They say she deserved it. And they teased me a lot that night about how much Prince Georgio liked me, but I noticed that they danced

with him just as often as I did. And
so did Isabella, Lucy and Ellie!

It was SUCH a fun evening.
The concert was lovely, with all
my favourite tunes, and when
Georgio brought out the golden
nightingale and wound it up it
was completely magical. As the
little golden bird began to sing
I could see first one and then
another of my friends rubbing
their eyes, and tears were
absolutely pouring down Fairy
G's face. The only people who
didn't think it the most beautiful
sound in the whole wide world
were Diamonde and Gruella.

They were standing to one side just looking bored – and do you know what? I felt sorry for them. Just imagine not being able to

appreciate that glorious silver voice trilling and warbling and filling your head with the most wonderful pictures...

The dancing was brilliant too. The twins were sent back to Pearl Palace before it began, so Prince Georgio didn't have to worry about them, and neither did we.

We whirled and twirled until we were dizzy, and laughed just about non-stop until the coaches rolled up to take us home.

"Thank you for a lovely evening," I said as Georgio came to say goodbye.

"Thank YOU, Grace," he said. "I haven't had so much fun in ages! Promise you'll come again?"

And I don't know if he was asking me, or all of Lily Room...but it would be fun to see him again. Friends need to see each other...and I do so hope we'll see you again very soon. Pearl Palace wouldn't be the same without YOU!

What happens next?
Find out in

and the Enchanted Fawn

Hello, and how are you?
I'm Princess Ellie, and I'm one of the
Lily Room princesses – but you probably
know that already if you've met my friends
Hannah, Isabella, Lucy, Grace and Sarah.
I do hope you have; they're SO lovely –
just like you! We have lots of fun
when we're together – as long
as the twins aren't around...

Look out for

Princess Parade

with Princess Hannah and Princess Lucy
ISBN 978 1 84616 504 7

And look out for the Daffodil Room princesses in
the Tiara Club at Emerald Castle:

Princess Amelia and the Silver Seal
Princess Leah and the Golden Seahorse
Princess Ruby and the Enchanted Whale
Princess Millie and the Magical Mermaid
Princess Rachel and the Dancing Dolphin
Princess Zoe and the Wishing Shell

The **Tiara** *Club*

Win a Tiara Club
Perfect Princess Prize!

Look for the secret word in mirror writing that is hidden in a tiara in each of the Tiara Club books. Each book has one word. Put together the six words from books **19** to **24** to make a special Perfect Princess sentence, then send it to us together with 20 words or more on why you like the Tiara Club books. Each month, we will put the correct entries in a draw and one lucky reader will receive a magical Perfect Princess prize!

Send your Perfect Princess sentence,
at least 20 words on why you like the Tiara Club,
your name and your address on a postcard to:
THE TIARA CLUB COMPETITION,
Orchard Books, 338 Euston Road,
London, NW1 3BH

Australian readers should write to:
Hachette Children's Books,
Level 17/207 Kent Street, Sydney, NSW 2000.

Only one entry per child.
Final draw: 30 September 2008

By Vivian French
Illustrated by Sarah Gibb

The Tiara Club

The Tiara Club at Silver Towers

The Tiara Club at Ruby Mansions

The Tiara Club at Pearl Palace

PRINCESS HANNAH <small>AND THE LITTLE BLACK KITTEN</small>	ISBN	978 1 84616 498 9
PRINCESS ISABELLA <small>AND THE SNOW-WHITE UNICORN</small>	ISBN	978 1 84616 499 6
PRINCESS LUCY <small>AND THE PRECIOUS PUPPY</small>	ISBN	978 1 84616 500 9
PRINCESS GRACE <small>AND THE GOLDEN NIGHTINGALE</small>	ISBN	978 1 84616 501 6
PRINCESS ELLIE <small>AND THE ENCHANTED FAWN</small>	ISBN	978 1 84616 502 3
PRINCESS SARAH <small>AND THE SILVER SWAN</small>	ISBN	978 1 84616 503 0
BUTTERFLY BALL	ISBN	978 1 84616 470 5
CHRISTMAS WONDERLAND	ISBN	978 1 84616 296 1
PRINCESS PARADE	ISBN	978 1 84616 504 7

All priced at £3.99.
Butterfly Ball, *Christmas Wonderland* and *Princess Parade* are priced at £5.99.
The Tiara Club books are available from all good bookshops, or can be ordered
direct from the publisher: Orchard Books, PO BOX 29, Douglas IM99 1BQ.
Credit card orders please telephone 01624 836000
or fax 01624 837033 or visit our website: www.orchardbooks.co.uk
or e-mail: bookshop@enterprise.net for details.

To order please quote title, author and ISBN and your full name and address.
Cheques and postal orders should be made payable to 'Bookpost plc.'
Postage and packing is FREE within the UK
(overseas customers should add £2.00 per book).

Prices and availability are subject to change.

Check out

The Tiara Club

website at:

www.tiaraclub.co.uk

You'll find Perfect Princess games and fun
things to do, as well as news on the Tiara
Club and all your favourite princesses!